# SOCCER
## Show-Off

### BY JAKE MADDOX

text by Margaret Gurevich
illustrated by Katie Wood

STONE ARCH BOOKS
a capstone imprint

Jake Maddox books are published by Stone Arch Books
A Capstone Imprint
1710 Roe Crest Drive
North Mankato, Minnesota 56003
www.capstonepub.com

Library of Congress Cataloging-in-Publication Data

Maddox, Jake, author.
Soccer show-off / by Jake Maddox ; text by Margaret Gurevich;
illustrated by Katie Wood.
pages cm. -- (Jake Maddox girl sports stories)
Summary: Gina tries to be the star of the soccer team at her
newschool, but her teammates do not like her showoff moves.
ISBN 978-1-4342-4144-3 (hardcover) -- ISBN 978-1-4342-7932-3 (pbk.)
-- ISBN 978-1-4342-9288-9 (eBook PDF)
1. Soccer stories. 2. Teamwork (Sports)--Juvenile fiction. 3.
Sportsmanship--Juvenile fiction. [1. Soccer--Fiction. 2. Teamwork
(Sports)--Fiction. 3. Sportsmanship--Fiction.] I. Gurevich, Margaret,
author. II. Wood, Katie, 1981- illustrator. III. Title.

PZ7.M25643Sob 2014
[Fic]--dc23

2013028662

Designer: Alison Thiele
Production Specialist: Charmaine Whitman

Printed in China.
092013
007735LEOS14

# TABLE OF CONTENTS

River City Middle School
HOME OF THE RIVER CITY RAIDERS
RIVER CITY MIDDLE SCHOOL

Chapter One

# NEW SCHOOL

Gina Gonzalez noticed the sign as soon as she approached River City Middle School. A banner that read "Home of the River City Raiders!" hung across the entrance.

Gina smiled. *That could be my new team,* she thought. *I could be a Raider!*

All around her, kids hurried into the building. Gina's stomach was tied in knots. River City Middle School was at least twice the size of her old school.

*All I have to do is make it through the day,* Gina thought. *Then I can go to soccer tryouts.*

Just then, the first bell rang. Gina pretended she was on the soccer field and pushed down the hall to her homeroom.

* * *

The end of the day could not come fast enough for Gina. As soon as the bell rang, she ran to her locker, put on her cleats, and headed for the soccer field behind the school.

At first, she was the only one there. Within minutes, groups of girls in red jerseys made their way onto the field. Some practiced passing. Others bounced the soccer balls on their knees or heads. They were all laughing and smiling, and Gina relaxed a little.

One of the girls closest to Gina smiled at her. "Hey, I'm Rachel," she said, smoothing her hair back into a ponytail. "You must be new."

Gina nodded. "Yep," she said. "I'm Gina."

"It's nice to meet you!" said Rachel. "Let me introduce you to some of the other girls."

Rachel turned and waved to some girls across the field. "New girl!" she called.

Rachel's friends immediately hurried over. "We love new girls," one of the girls said happily. "I'm Becca, by the way."

"I'm Lara," said another. "I'm glad you're trying out. We could use some new players to spice things up. We hardly won any games last season."

Gina bounced on her toes and clutched her ball. "I'll do my best," she promised.

"That's all I can ask of my players," a voice behind Gina said. "For them to do their best."

Gina turned around and saw a tall woman holding a whistle and a clipboard. The woman raised her whistle and blew it sharply. The rest of the players immediately came running in.

Gina followed the lead of the other girls as they sat in a circle in the middle of the field.

"For those who don't know me, I'm Coach Grant," the woman said. "During today's tryouts, I'll be looking for each of your strengths and to see how you'll work with the team."

"We'll start with passing today," Coach Grant continued. "Pair up, and let's see what you can do."

Gina turned to Rachel. "Want to be partners?" she asked hopefully.

"Sure," Rachel said with a grin. "We're going to rock this."

Coach Grant tossed several soccer balls onto the field. One of the balls landed at Gina's feet, and she stopped it with her instep. In one smooth motion, she passed it to Rachel.

"Nice work!" called Coach Grant from the sidelines, and Gina beamed.

Rachel stopped the ball and used the inside of her foot to pass it back to Gina.

"Way to work those feet, girls," the coach called.

Gina tapped the ball with her toes. Then she passed it back to Rachel. After they'd practiced passing for several more minutes, Coach Grant blew her whistle to get their attention.

"Okay, let's split into two groups to practice dribbling," the coach shouted. She motioned for Gina, Rachel, and a few other girls to go first. "Take it down the field, ladies!"

Gina and the other girls each grabbed a ball and dribbled down the pitch. Gina made sure to keep the ball under control, tapping it back and forth between her feet as she ran.

"Very nice, girls! Bring it in!" Coach Grant shouted as they reached the end of the field.

While Gina, Rachel, and the other six girls rested on the sidelines, the next group ran to the field. Gina saw the coach write something in her notebook.

"You better breathe, or you'll pass out," said a voice beside Gina.

Gina jumped. It was only Rachel, but Gina had been concentrating so hard on the field, she hadn't heard her come up beside her.

"I'm a little nervous," Gina admitted.

Rachel nodded. "Me too, but you were awesome out there," she said. "You can really control the ball."

"Thanks," said Gina, blushing.

Coach blew her whistle again. "Nice job, everyone. Time to do some power kicking. Line 'em up!" she said.

All the girls ran to the field. Coach Grant got into position in front of the net to play goalie. Each time the coach blew her whistle, a new girl ran to kick the ball into the net.

When it was Gina's turn, she took aim and kicked the ball with a powerful *thwack!* The ball sailed past Coach Grant's fingers and into the net.

"Great kick!" Rachel said as Gina jogged to the back of the line.

"Okay, let's take turns acting as goalie now," Coach Grant called.

Gina cringed. She was a terrible goalie. When it was her turn, she stared intently at the ball, trying to figure out its path. She threw her body into each block. But she couldn't even save half the shots.

"Don't worry," Rachel told her afterward. "Besides, goalie is kind of my thing. What we really need is someone to score goals."

Gina was starting to feel better when Lara joined them.

"You were great out there," Lara said. "Coach would be crazy not to put you on the team."

"Thanks," said Gina, smiling. She just hoped they were right.

Chapter Two

# A NEW TEAM

The next day at school, Gina's stomach was in knots. The team list was supposed to be up at the end of the day. As soon as the final bell rang, Gina bolted from her classroom. When she got to the gym, Rachel, Lara, and Becca were already waiting.

"You're as antsy as we are," said Lara.

"I could barely focus all day," said Gina.

Becca laughed. "That makes four of us!" she said.

Finally, the gym doors swung open, and the girls all pushed inside to look at the list.

Rachel got there first, and Gina heard her squeal excitedly.

"We all made it!" said Rachel. "I knew we would!"

Rachel pulled Gina, Becca, and Lara into a huddle, and the girls jumped up and down. Just then, Coach Grant walked into the gym.

"Welcome, Raiders!" the coach said. "I'm very excited about the new faces on the team this year."

Gina and the others cheered.

"But," continued Coach Grant, "we have lots of practice to do before our first scrimmage this week."

The coach kept talking, but Gina was only half listening. She was already picturing herself running across the field, passing the ball, and scoring goals with her power kicks.

In the distance, she heard the coach talking about teamwork and helping each other, but Gina kept daydreaming. Suddenly, she felt a sharp elbow poke her in the ribs.

"Wake up," Rachel whispered. "Coach wants us to run through some drills."

Gina blushed and followed Rachel into the locker room to get changed. She didn't want Coach to think she couldn't focus.

Once they were out on the field, Rachel and Gina paired up again.

"Ready?" asked Rachel.

Gina nodded. "Yep, let's go!" she called back.

Rachel bent her right knee slightly and used the inside of her foot to strike the center of the ball. She made sure to follow through with her kicking foot so that the inside of her foot ended facing Gina.

The ball zoomed quickly toward Gina, and she moved toward it to trap it with her toe.

"Nice!" Rachel called from the opposite end of the field.

Just then Coach Grant made her way to the girls.

*I'm going to show her my special moves,* Gina thought. *She'll have to be impressed when I show her how high I can kick the ball with the chip pass.*

Gina placed her right toe at the bottom of the soccer ball and put her other foot against its side. Then she lifted the ball with her toe and sent it soaring through the air toward Rachel.

Rachel gave Gina a questioning look but stepped back and let the ball bounce off her chest. "Take it easy," she called.

"Good job, girls," Coach Grant said. "But I want you to focus on a simple dribbling and passing routine for now. Those are the most important skills in our games."

Gina frowned, but did what the coach wanted for the rest of the practice.

*Besides, I'll have plenty of time to help the team at Friday's game*, Gina thought confidently.

Chapter Three

# THE FIRST GAME

"Is everyone ready for some soccer?"
Coach Grant asked the team at their first
game Friday afternoon. They were playing
the Tigers, a team from a nearby middle
school.

"Yeah!" the Raiders cheered excitedly
from the sidelines.

"Remember," the coach said, "watch
the ball, the other team, and your own
teammates. Teamwork is key."

Gina bounced with excitement. She couldn't wait to get on the field and play a real game.

The referee threw a coin in the air, and the field was silent as everyone waited for it to come down.

"Heads," the referee said when the coin landed. "Kickoff goes to the Tigers."

The Raiders groaned but got into position on the field. The Tigers' center midfielder stepped up for the kickoff. She kicked the ball lightly to the midfielder on her left, who immediately passed it back.

The second the ball touched her cleat again, the center midfielder took off up the field, dribbling the ball between her feet as she ran. Gina and Becca, who were both playing midfield, hustled after her.

Gina watched the other player's feet as she tried to figure out the best way to steal the ball. Becca caught Gina's eye, and Gina moved her head slightly to show they should close in on the Tiger.

Becca ran faster, racing up on the Tiger's left while Gina closed in on the right. But the Tigers' player was in tune with her surroundings. Just when Gina made a move for the ball, the other player passed the ball up the field to one of the Tigers' forwards.

Lara, playing defense, tried to get in front of the ball. The Tigers' forward was getting too close to the Raiders' goal. But the Tigers moved quickly, and Rachel didn't stand a chance. The ball grazed her shoulder and landed inside the goal. The Tigers were up by one, and it was the Raiders' turn to kick off.

Becca took the kickoff and passed it to Gina. She dribbled it down the field, keeping an eye on the Tigers' offense. One of the Tigers' midfielders crowded her, and Gina looked for an open Raiders' player to pass to.

She spotted Amy, one of the other midfielders, and kicked the ball across the field to her. Amy dribbled the ball between the Tigers' defense, getting closer to the goal. But suddenly, one of the Tigers' defenders swooped in, knocking the ball away. Luckily, Becca broke free and managed to recover the ball.

Becca moved closer to the goal, trying to find a clear shot. *Thwack!* She sent the ball soaring past the Tigers' goalie and into the net. The Raiders hugged each other and jumped up and down. They were tied 1-1.

There were still three minutes left in the first half, and the Raiders were back in the game. Unfortunately, the Tigers had the ball. The Tigers' coach called a time-out, and Gina watched as they huddled up to discuss their strategy.

*I wonder what they're planning*, she thought.

Gina moved over to where Becca and Amy stood. "We need to be on top of our passing," said Gina.

"Agreed," Becca said.

The referee blew the whistle, and the game started up again. As soon as the ball was back in play, Gina, Becca, and Amy zoomed in on the Tigers' forward with the ball, but she managed to pass to one of her teammates.

Then the forward tried to sprint around the Raiders' players to complete the pass. The Raiders tried to cover her, but she was too fast.

Gina tried to focus, but she was frustrated. *All this teamwork is slowing us down*, she thought. *I wish I could just run down the field myself and score a goal.*

There were only five seconds left in the first half, and the Tigers knew how to time it. One of their forwards took aim and kicked the ball toward the Raiders' goal.

Rachel couldn't make the save. The ball sailed into the net just as the whistle blew to signal the end of the first half.

The Raiders were losing.

Chapter Four

# BALL HOG

"Okay, girls, good work out there, but I need my defense to work together," Coach Grant told them during halftime. "Offense, make sure you stay on the Tigers. Don't give them any breathing room to pass."

Gina nodded. *Got it*, she thought. *No breathing room. I'll be right there every time.*

The Raiders had the ball at the start of the second half. Becca took the kickoff and passed the ball to Gina.

As soon as the ball touched her feet, Gina took control and dribbled down the field. She faked a pass and darted around a midfielder.

The Tigers' defenders were closing in on her. From the corner of her eye, Gina caught a glimpse of Lara, who was wide open. Still, Gina held onto the ball.

From the sidelines, Coach Grant yelled, "Pass! Pass!"

But Gina was determined to show the coach that she could do it herself. *Now or never*, she thought.

Gina took aim and kicked the ball, sending it up into the air. It curved toward the goal, out of the goalie's reach, and sailed into the back of the net. Score! The Raiders and Tigers were tied.

Gina saw the rest of the Raiders grinning too. She knew she'd done the right thing by not passing the ball. Everyone wanted to win as much as she did.

The Tigers took the next kickoff, and Gina watched as the player dribbled the ball down the field. She kept the ball securely between her feet, and Gina could tell stealing it away wouldn't be easy.

Out of the corner of her eye, Gina saw Becca moving toward the opposing player too, but she blocked her way.

*What if Becca misses?* Gina thought. *I better just do it.*

Gina stole the ball and made a break for the goal. The Tigers' defenders surrounded her, and she heard Lara yell, "I'm open! Pass!"

Gina ignored her teammate and kept running. She kicked hard — goal! Gina grinned happily. The Raiders were winning, and there were only two minutes left in the game.

*If I can just stay on the ball, we'll definitely win*, thought Gina.

"Let me in there too, okay?" Becca whispered as the play began.

Gina nodded, but as soon as the ball was back in play, she took off. She wanted to keep the ball away from their goal. Rachel was a good goalie, but the Tigers seemed to know all her tricks.

One of the Tigers' forwards passed the ball to her teammate, who dribbled toward the net. The Raiders' defenders looked ready, but Gina didn't want to chance it.

Just as Lara got close to the Tigers' player with the ball, Gina ran in and booted it away. Lara stumbled, and the whistle blew to end the game.

"We won!" Gina shouted. "We won!"

The rest of her teammates gave each other high fives, but they didn't seem as excited as Gina had expected.

"Why's everyone so down?" she asked.

Lara glared at Gina. "Maybe we'd feel a little better if you let someone else have a turn." She turned and walked off the field, bumping Gina's shoulder as she passed.

Gina looked at Becca. "What's up with her?" she asked.

Becca sighed. "You're not the only player on the team, you know," she said, shaking her head.

Gina couldn't understand why the Raiders were acting this way. She knew Coach Grant would understand.

Gina jogged over to her coach. "Good game, huh?" she said.

But the look on Coach Grant's face said she didn't agree. "I'm glad you're enthusiastic, Gina," she replied. "You're certainly talented. But you need to remember that soccer is a team sport."

Gina frowned. Didn't the team want to win as much as she did? Didn't her coach want that too?

*Why don't they want my help?* she wondered.

Chapter Five

# SHOWING OFF

Three days later, the Raiders were back on the field for their next game. This time they were playing the Mariners.

Gina looked around at her teammates. Everyone was in a good mood today. Unlike after the first game, no one was acting annoyed with her.

*Maybe everyone was just tired at the end of the game*, Gina thought. She knew she could get grumpy after a long, tiring game.

"Remember, ladies," Coach Grant was saying, "we can win this one as long as we work as a team."

"If all of us work together, we can definitely win," Becca whispered to Gina.

Gina nodded excitedly. She was all for working together . . . as long as the Raiders won.

The referee blew the whistle, and the Raiders and Mariners gathered for the kickoff. Lara kicked the ball down the field, and Becca stopped it with her knee.

"Keep on it, Becca!" Coach Grant shouted.

Gina stayed close to Becca, making sure to keep herself open. When one of the Mariners' players got close to Becca, she passed the ball to Gina.

Gina dribbled the ball down the field and remembered to pass it to Lara. Lara stayed on the ball, bringing it in close to the net. She kicked it past the defenders. Goal!

"That's the teamwork I'm taking about!" Coach Grant shouted. "Keep it up, ladies!"

The Raiders jumped up and down, but didn't have long to celebrate. The Mariners took possession of the ball and got to work moving it down the field.

Gina was impressed with their speed. The Tigers would have to stick to the Mariners like glue if they wanted to stop them. Becca made a move to steal the ball away, but the Mariners' player was too quick. She did a swift backward pass, sending the ball to a teammate behind her with the sole of her cleat.

*They're good, but we need to be better*, Gina thought.

Gina tried to get ahead of the Mariners' player controlling the ball, but the other girl was too quick. Almost before Gina knew what had happened, the girl dodged around her and lobbed the ball into the Raiders' goal.

The rest of the Mariners cheered as the ball hit the back of the net. The game was now tied 1-1. Both Rachel and the defense looked irritated.

"Shake it off," Coach Grant called. "Focus, girls!"

"We have the ball now," Gina said to Becca. "Let's make sure we keep it."

Becca grinned. "My plan exactly," she agreed.

The game was on again, and the Raiders stayed on the ball. They had their passing down, and Gina did her best to stay open. Lara passed the ball to her, and Gina dribbled down the field.

"Pass, Gina!" Coach Grant shouted from the sidelines.

Gina passed the ball up the field to Becca, who took off, weaving in and out of the Mariners. When a Mariner snuck up beside her and made a move for the ball, she passed it back to Gina.

Gina could see the goal up ahead. She wanted to score and put the Raiders in the lead. Suddenly, a Mariners' defender was at her side. Gina knew it was risky, but she refused to give up the ball. She wanted to make that goal.

"I'm open!" she heard Amy yell.

"Pass the ball!" Coach Grant shouted.

Gina ignored them and dribbled faster. *I can do it*, she thought stubbornly.

But suddenly a Mariners' defender swiped the ball away and kicked it up the field in the opposite direction. A Mariners' midfielder quickly ran after the ball and started dribbling toward the Raiders' goal. The defense was there, but they weren't fast enough. Goal!

The first period was over. The Mariners were up by one, and the Raiders were glaring at Gina like it was all her fault.

Chapter Six

# RIDING THE BENCH

At the start of the second half, the Raiders did not look happy. Several of the girls glared at Gina.

*I don't get it,* Gina thought. *All I want to do is help. Sometimes the ball gets stolen. It's not like it only happens to me.*

Gina sighed and adjusted her shin guards. She had to do better this period.

"Gina, wait a second," Coach Grant said as Gina started to jog onto the field.

Gina stopped. "What's up, Coach?" she asked.

"I want you to sit out the rest of the game," the coach said.

Gina couldn't believe what she was hearing. "What?" she said. "But why?"

"This team isn't about one person," Coach Grant said. "It's about teamwork. Everyone has skills they're good at. The purpose of a team is to let everyone do her part."

Gina felt tears prick her eyes as she walked over to the bench and sat down. She'd never been asked to sit out a game before. She couldn't believe it. Gina stared stubbornly at the ground, kicking the grass and refusing to look at what was happening on the field.

But when she heard people cheering in the bleachers, Gina couldn't stand it anymore. She looked up. The Raiders had control of the ball and were moving it down the field.

Gina saw Carrie, a girl she'd never watched before, pass the ball to Lara. Carrie's pass went straight to Lara's feet like they were magnets.

Gina frowned. *Why haven't I noticed how good Carrie is before?* she wondered.

Gina's eyes stayed glued to the field as Lara kicked the ball off the ground and into the air in front of the goal. All of a sudden, Becca came charging to the center as well. She jumped up in the air and angled her body, heading the ball into the net. Tie game again!

Gina glanced at the clock. There were only two minutes left. She looked back at the field. In the goal, Rachel looked ready for anything.

Becca, Lara, and Carrie all stayed close to the Mariners' players they were guarding, making sure they couldn't pass the ball. It seemed like the Raiders had their system down pat.

*I wonder if it looks like that when I'm on the field*, Gina thought. *It sure doesn't feel like it.*

Then it hit her. Things didn't flow as smoothly because she was too busy trying to shine on her own.

The clock was running down, and the Mariners still had the ball. They were getting closer to the Raiders' goal each second.

Gina watched as her teammates tried to surround the Mariners' player with the ball, but she zoomed around them. The goal was inches away. The Mariners' forward shot as the buzzer sounded. Goal! The Mariners won the game.

After the Raiders finished shaking hands with the Mariners, Gina snuck off to the bus. She picked a single seat in the back and put her headphones on. She didn't want to talk to anyone on the team. Not when she knew she'd cost the Raiders the game.

# Chapter Seven

# ODD GIRL OUT

The next morning, Gina thought about staying home sick. It wouldn't have been a lie. The thought of facing her teammates made her sick to her stomach.

*Maybe I can pretend to be sick and go to the nurse's office if they're as mad at me as I think,* Gina decided.

Gina's stomach was filled with butterflies as she walked into school. As she got closer to her locker, she saw Becca waiting for her.

*I hope she's not here to yell at me,* Gina thought nervously. *Or that she at least gets it over with quickly.*

"Hey," Gina said quietly.

"Hi," said Becca. "I came to see how you were doing. You didn't sit with us on the bus ride home."

Gina felt her eyes fill with tears. "I didn't think you'd want me to," she said. "I know everyone hates me. I let the whole team down."

Becca shook her head. "No one hates you, Gina," she said. "They're just frustrated."

Gina wiped at her eyes and looked down at the dingy floor of the hallway. "I know," she said. "Because we lost. It's all my fault. I'm really sorry."

Becca put her hand on Gina's arm. "It's not because we lost," Becca said. "I mean, no one was thrilled with that, but it's not like it was the first time. We're upset because we all like to play."

Gina was confused. "I just want to help," she said.

Becca sighed. "I know, and that's great. But we're all on the team because, duh, we love soccer!" she said with a smile.

Gina smiled back. "Yeah, I get it," she said. "I wasn't giving anyone else a chance to do what they love."

"Exactly," Becca said. "One person can't carry the whole team. It's too much pressure and work. If we win, we do it together."

Gina laughed a little. "And if we lose, we do that together too," she said.

Becca laughed in agreement. "You got it," she said.

"Thanks," said Gina. "You're a good friend."

"Sit with us at lunch today," Becca suggested, "and you'll see that the other Raiders are good friends too."

# Chapter Eight

# PLAYING AS A TEAM

Gina felt nervous as she walked over to join her teammates at lunch. But she shouldn't have worried. They seemed to have forgiven her. They gave her a hard time about hogging the ball, but they laughed while doing it.

But practice that afternoon was a different story. Not all the Raiders had been at the lunch table. Gina would have to face them for the first time since yesterday's loss.

As she walked toward the soccer field with Becca after school, Gina noticed some of the other players glaring at her.

"I don't think the rest of the team is quite as ready to forgive me," Gina mumbled. "They look mad."

Rachel ran up beside her. "What are you talking about?" she asked as she joined them.

"Gina is worried the team is still mad at her," Becca explained.

Rachel put her arm around Gina's other shoulder. "That's crazy talk," she said. She made her voice deep like Coach Grant's. "Besides, that's not how we work as a team."

All the girls giggled, and Gina felt relieved.

"Now let's show everyone what working as a team can do," Becca said. She grabbed Gina's hand and pulled her onto the field.

The girls split up into two lines and worked on the give-and-go drill. One player from each line ran toward the goal, passing the ball back and forth as they ran. Rachel took her place at the goal while the rest of the Raiders took turns shooting.

After they finished their drills, the girls split into two teams for a scrimmage. Gina focused on her footwork but made sure to keep an eye on her teammates as she played. Whenever she was cornered, she passed the ball to an open player.

At the end of practice, no one gave Gina the cold shoulder. Coach Grant gathered the girls and smiled wider than Gina had ever seen.

"I'm really proud of all of you," she said. "That was the best teamwork I've seen in a long time. At Friday's game, I have no doubt we'll show just how good our skills are."

# Chapter Nine

# BACK IN THE GAME

The rest of the week flew by. Before Gina knew it, it was time for Friday's game. She couldn't wait to play again. She met Becca, Lara, and Rachel by the gym, and they all walked to the field together.

"I can't wait to get out on the field!" Gina exclaimed.

"We're so going to win," Rachel added.

"Don't forget the teamwork, ladies," Coach Grant said, walking up behind them.

"Can't forget that!" Gina agreed.

The Raiders saw the other team, the Panthers, already on the field. Everyone hurried to get into position as well.

The Raiders took the kickoff, and Gina dribbled the ball down the field. The heat was on, and the Panthers' players were on her heels.

Gina quickly looked around the field and made eye contact with Becca. Gina kicked a chip pass over the other players to her. Becca knocked the ball down to the ground with her chest.

The crowd cheered as Becca moved closer to the goal. She was almost there, but the Panthers' defense blocked her. Lara was on it, swooping in from the outside to kick the ball in. 1-0, Raiders!

The Panthers wasted no time getting their feet on the ball. Gina watched as they used fancy kicks and footwork to move the ball toward the Raiders' goal. The defenders worked to block the goal, but the Panthers' forward managed to kick it in. The game was tied 1-1.

As they moved into the second half, Gina could tell the rest of the Raiders were anxious too. They wanted to win as much as she did. And they'd have to work together to do it.

The Raiders took turns dribbling the ball down the field. They got close to the Panthers' goal several times, but the Panthers' defense always managed to deflect the ball. Luckily for the Raiders, the Panthers were in the same position. The Raiders' defense stopped them cold.

With only two minutes left in the game, the Raiders had possession of the ball again. This time, Carrie dribbled the ball down the field. Her feet moved quickly as they pushed the ball, but the Panthers swarmed in.

Carrie kicked the ball over to Gina, who knocked it to the ground with her chest. The seconds ticked away, and Gina ran down the field.

The goal loomed before her, and Gina could taste the win. The Panthers could too. They swooped in to steal the ball away, but Gina did a backward pass to Lara before that could happen.

Lara pulled her leg back to kick the ball into the goal, but a Panthers' defender stood in her way. She quickly passed the ball back to Gina.

The clock flashed ten seconds. Gina looked around to see if there was an open teammate to pass to.

"Shoot!" yelled Becca. "There's no time."

Gina swallowed, pulled her leg back, and shot the ball high into the air. Goal!

Gina barely registered what had happened before the other Raiders swarmed her. Everyone was cheering with excitement.

"You did it!" Rachel hollered.

Gina grinned. This was what she'd wanted from the moment she joined the Raiders. But something was different now. She looked at her teammates and Coach Grant. She hadn't scored that goal alone. They'd worked together up until the last second.

"No," Gina said, "we did it — together!"

# Author Bio

Margaret Gurevich has wanted to be a writer since second grade. She has written for many magazines and currently writes young adult and middle grade books. She lives with her husband, son, and two furry kitties and fondly remembers her cheerleading days.

# Illustrator Bio

Katie Wood fell in love with drawing when she was very small. Since graduating from Loughborough University School of Art and Design in 2004, she has been living her dream working as a freelance illustrator. From her studio in Leicester, England, she creates bright and lively illustrations for books and magazines all over the world.

# Glossary

**CELEBRATE** (SEL-uh-brate) — to do something enjoyable on a special occasion

**DETERMINED** (di-TUR-mind) — feeling firm in your decision to do something

**DINGY** (DIN-jee) — dull and dirty

**ENTHUSIASTIC** (en-thoo-zee-ASS-tik) — very excited about or interested in something

**FOCUS** (FOH-kuss) — to concentrate on something or somebody

**PRESSURE** (PRESH-ur) — strong influence, force, or persuasion

**SCRIMMAGE** (SKRIM-ij) — a game played for practice in sports

**STRATEGY** (STRAT-uh-jee) — a clever plan for winning a military battle or achieving a goal

# Discussion Questions

**1.** How would you feel after the first game if you were one of Gina's new teammates on the Raiders? Talk about it.

**2.** Do you think it was fair of the coach to bench Gina because of how she played? Talk about why or why not.

**3.** Why do you think Gina was so determined to show off in the beginning of this book? Discuss some possible reasons.

# Writing Prompts

**1.** Gina is nervous on her first day at her new school. Have you ever started a new school? Write a paragraph about how you felt.

**2.** Imagine that you're Becca. Write a paragraph about what kind of advice you would give to Gina.

**3.** Which position would you like to play in soccer? Write about your choice.

# Soccer Positions

**DEFENDER** — this player plays in front of the goal and is focused on stopping the opposing team from scoring

**FORWARD** — the player in front of the rest of the team who takes the most shots and is responsible for most of the team's scoring

**FULLBACK** — a rear defender

**GOALKEEPER** — the player positioned in the goal to block the opposing team's shots

**MIDFIELDER** — the player in the middle of the field between the forwards and defenders; this position links defense and offense through ball control and passing

**STRIKER** — a team's main scoring player; similar to a forward

**SWEEPER** — a single defender who plays directly in front of the goal

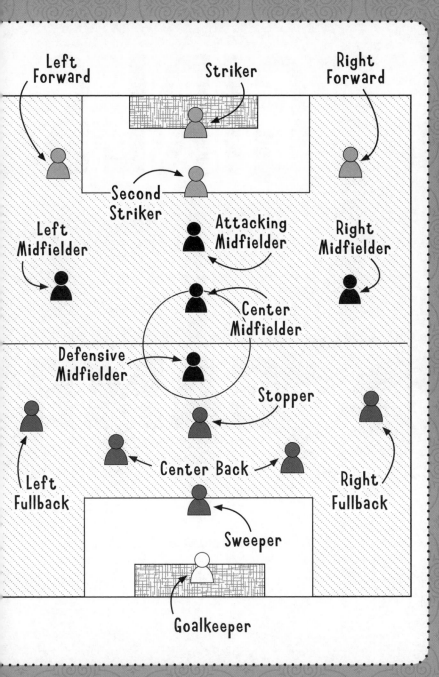

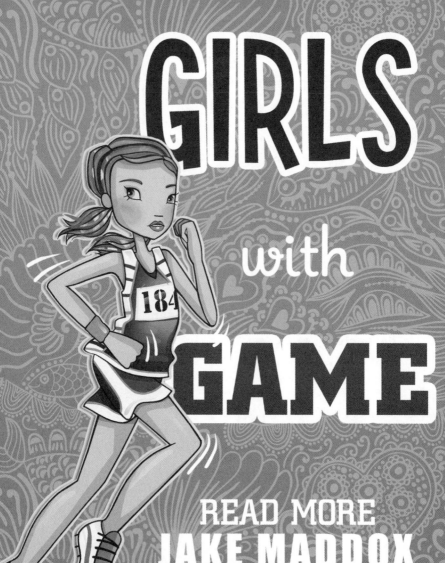

GIRLS

with

GAME

READ MORE
**JAKE MADDOX**
STORIES!

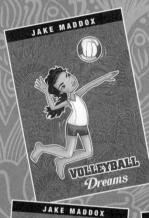

JAKE MADDOX

VOLLEYBALL
*Dreams*

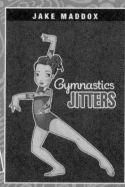

JAKE MADDOX

*Gymnastics*
**JITTERS**

JAKE MADDOX

**SOCCER
SURPRISE**

JAKE MADDOX

**REBOUND
TIME**

JAKE MADDOX

*Running*
**SCARED**

JAKE MADDOX

**HORSEBACK**
*Hurdles*

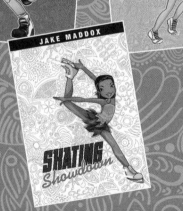

JAKE MADDOX

**SKATING**
*Showdown*

JAKE MADDOX

DANCE TEAM
**DILEMMA**